MARCUS PFISTER

RAINBOW FISH
AND THE WHALE

NorthSouth
New York / London

A long way out in the deep blue sea, Rainbow Fish swam happily with his friends.

The water was full of delicious food called krill.
When he was hungry, all Rainbow Fish had to do
was open his mouth to catch as much as he wanted.
It was a wonderful life.

One day a gentle old whale swam by and decided to stay. He too liked krill, and there was plenty here for everyone. And he liked to watch the pretty little fish with their glittering scales.

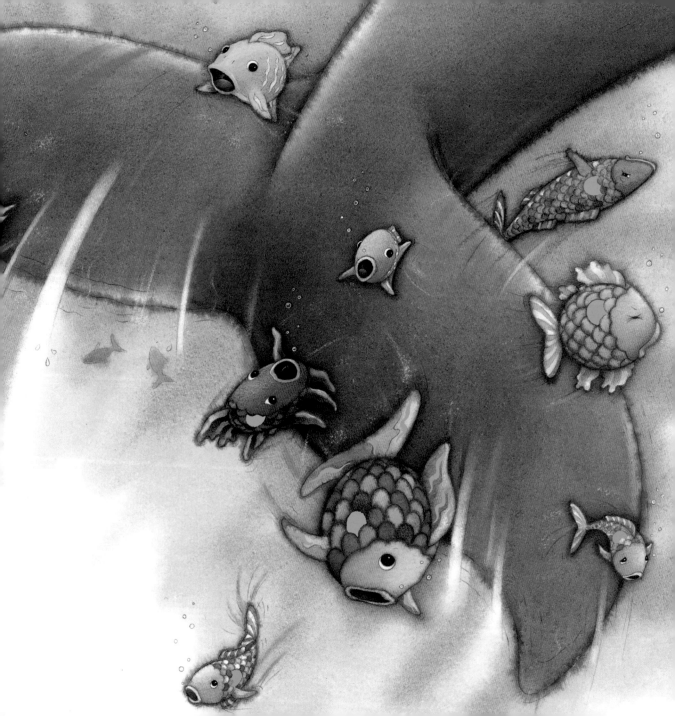

The terrified fish raced for safety to their cave.
But the whale followed them.

The old whale swam back and forth outside the cave.
The little fish were trapped!
"I told you he was dangerous!" said the orange fish.

Finally the whale calmed down and swam away. By then the little fish were very hungry. But when they left the cave, all the krill had been driven off.

"This is silly," said Rainbow Fish. "Before we were happy. Now we hide in a cave. Before there was plenty of krill for everyone. Now there is none. We have to make friends with the whale."

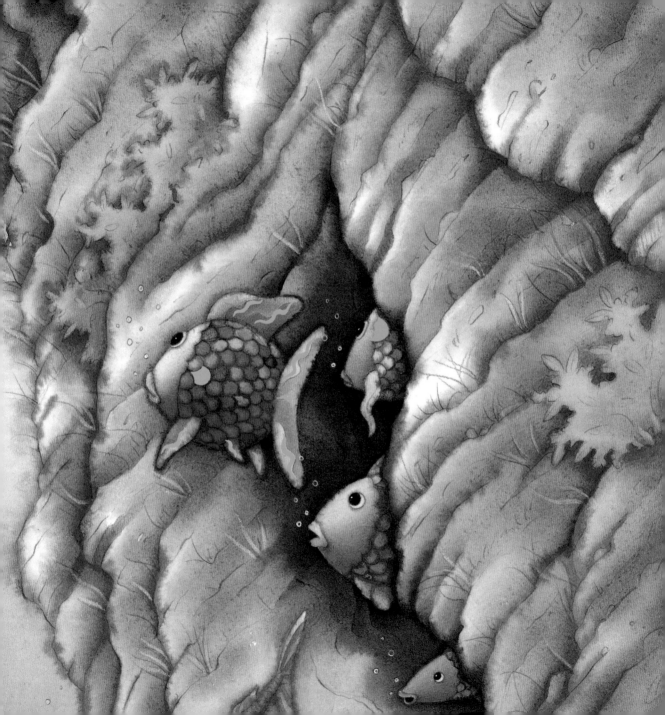

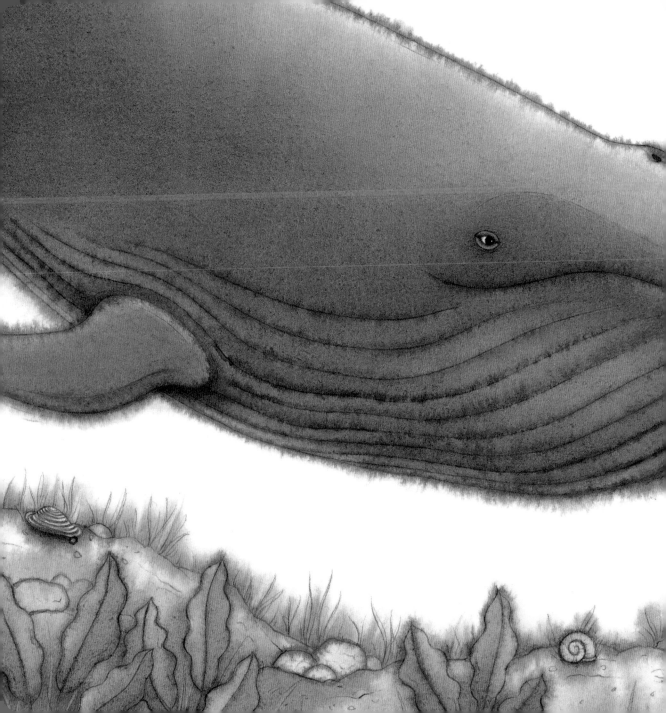

The other fish were all afraid to get close to the whale, so it was up to Rainbow Fish.

"Please, let's talk," said Rainbow Fish. "This fight was all a big mistake. It drove off the krill and now we're all hungry."

The whale told Rainbow Fish how their mean words had hurt him and made him angry. Rainbow Fish told the whale how frightened they were when the whale kept watching them.

"We thought you might want to eat us," said Rainbow Fish.

The whale was surprised. "I only watched you because you are so pretty," he said.

They both laughed.

"Come along now," said the whale. "Let's find some new hunting grounds."